Easter Bunny's On His Way!

by Brian James
Illustrated by Dara Goldman

SCHOLASTIC INC.
New York Toronto London Auckland Sydney
Mexico City New Delhi Hong Kong Buenos Aires

To Lynne
—D.G.

ISBN 0-439-74530-6

Text copyright © 2005 by Brian James.
Illustrations copyright © 2005 by Dara Goldman.
All rights reserved. Published by Scholastic Inc.
SCHOLASTIC and associated logos are trademarks
and/or registered trademarks of Scholastic Inc.

12 11 10 9 8 7 6 5 4 3   6 7 8 9 10/0

Printed in the U.S.A.
First printing, March 2005

Hooray!
The Easter Bunny's on his way!

We'll be painting lots of eggs before he comes!

We'll be painting lots of eggs before he comes!

We'll be painting lots of eggs,
We'll be painting lots of eggs,

We'll be painting lots of eggs
before he comes!

He'll be bringing lots of candy
when he comes!
He'll be bringing lots of candy
when he comes!

He'll be bringing lots of candy,
He'll be bringing lots of candy,
He'll be bringing lots of candy
when he comes!

He'll be hiding eggs all over
when he comes!
He'll be hiding eggs all over
when he comes!

He'll be hiding eggs all over,
He'll be hiding eggs all over,
He'll be hiding eggs all over
when he comes!

Oh, we'll all run out to see him when he comes!

Oh, we'll all run out to
see him when he comes!

Oh, we'll all run out to see him,
Oh, we'll all run out to see him,

Oh, we'll all run out to see him
when he comes!

And we'll all eat lots of chocolate when he's gone!

And we'll all eat lots of chocolate
when he's gone!

And we'll all eat lots of chocolate,
And we'll all eat lots of chocolate,

And we'll all eat lots of chocolate when he's gone!

We'll be paint—ing lots of eggs be—fore he comes!

We'll be paint—ing lots of eggs be—fore he comes!

We'll be paint—ing lots of eg—gs. We'll be paint—ing lots of

eg—gs. We'll be paint—ing lots of eggs be—fore he comes!

THANK YOU, EASTER BUNNY!